How do you like ou

We would really appreciate you leaving us a review.

Other Picture Books:

For other fun Picture Books by Kampelstone,
simply search for:

Kampelstone Picture Books

FACTS ABOUT EUROPEAN CHRISTMAS

- The German Weihnachtspyramide (Christmas pyramid) comes from the Ore Mountains (Erzgebirge) region in the German state of Sachsen. In the late 1700's, they were initially developed as a low-cost substitute for actual Christmas trees. These rotating, conically shaped wooden devices had up to five levels which contained carved figures, animals, trees or other decorations. Heat from candles around the base of the pyramid powers the fan at the top which then makes the whole structure rotate.

- Although there are hints that Christmas trees were decorated as early as 1441 in Tallinn, Estonia, the first actual record of a decorated Christmas Tree was written in 1510 in Riga, Latvia. At Christmas-time, members of the Merchants' Guild called the Brotherhood of the Black Heads paraded a tree decorated with dried roses, fruits, straw figures and ribbons through the town square. After dancing around the tree, they set fire to it.

- The first nativity scene was constructed in 1223 by Saint Francis of Assisi. He built it in a cave near Greccio, Italy and it contained a manger of hay as well as two live animals; a donkey and an ox.

- Martin Luther, the 16th-century Protestant reformer, was the first to add lighted candles to a tree at Christmas time. While walking home one evening in December, he was amazed by the brightly twinkling stars through the evergreen trees. In order to recreate the image for his family, he set up a tree and wired lit candles to the branches.

- At Christmas-time in the late 1600's, Austrians would cut off the tops of evergreen trees and hang them upside down in their living rooms. They would then decorate them with red ribbons, apples, nuts and sweet candies. The sweet ornaments be came so popular that the Christmas trees were referred to as "Sugar-trees".

- Advent calendars as we know them today developed over time, but one of the earliest records of a type of calendar is described in a children's book written by Elise Averdieck in 1851: Each evening, starting on the first of December, when Elizabeth, the main character in the book, goes to bed, her mother tacks up a picture on the wallpaper and the children know that when twenty four pictures are hanging on the wallpaper, then Christmas has arrived. When Gerhard Lang was young, his mother made a calendar with 24 candies attached to the lid of a cardboard box; one for each day before Christmas. As an adult, Gerhard worked at a lithograph company where he designed and printed the first commercial Advent calendar in 1908.

- During the Middle Ages in Northern Europe, people used evergreen wreaths with candles during the Christmas season to mark off the weeks before Christmas. The evergreen boughs and the circular shape were symbols for ongoing life.

- Tinsel was first created in 1610 in Nuremberg, Germany. The trees were strewn with lit candles and then people would hang thin ribbons of silver on the branches to reflect the candlelight.

- The iconic Christmas nutcracker depicting a standing soldier was first made in 1872 by Friedrich Wilhelm Füchtner, a craftsman in the Erzgebirge region of eastern Germany.

- Santa Claus, the old man of Christmas, goes by many names and traditions in the various countries of Europe:

- Austria — St Nikolaus
- Belgium — Kerstman (Christmas man)
- Czech Republic — Mikuláš
- Denmark — Julemanden (Christmas Man)
- England — Father Christmas
- Estonia — Jõuluvana (Old Man of Christmas)
- France — Le Père Noël (Father Christmas)
- Germany — Weihnachtsmann (Christmas Man)
- Greece — Άγιος Βασίλειος ο Μέγας (Saint Basil the Great)
- Italy — Babbo Natale (Father Christmas)
- Latvia — Ziemassvētku vecītis (Father Christmas)
- Lithuania — Kalėdų Senelis (Grandfather Christmas)
- Luxembourg — Kleeschen (St Nicholas)
- Netherlands — Kerstman (Christmas Man)
- Norway — Julenissen (Christmas Gnome)
- Poland — Gwiazdor (Star Man)
- Sweden — Jultomten (Christmas Gnome)
- Switzerland — Samichlaus
- Ukraine — Дід Мороз (Grandfather Frost)

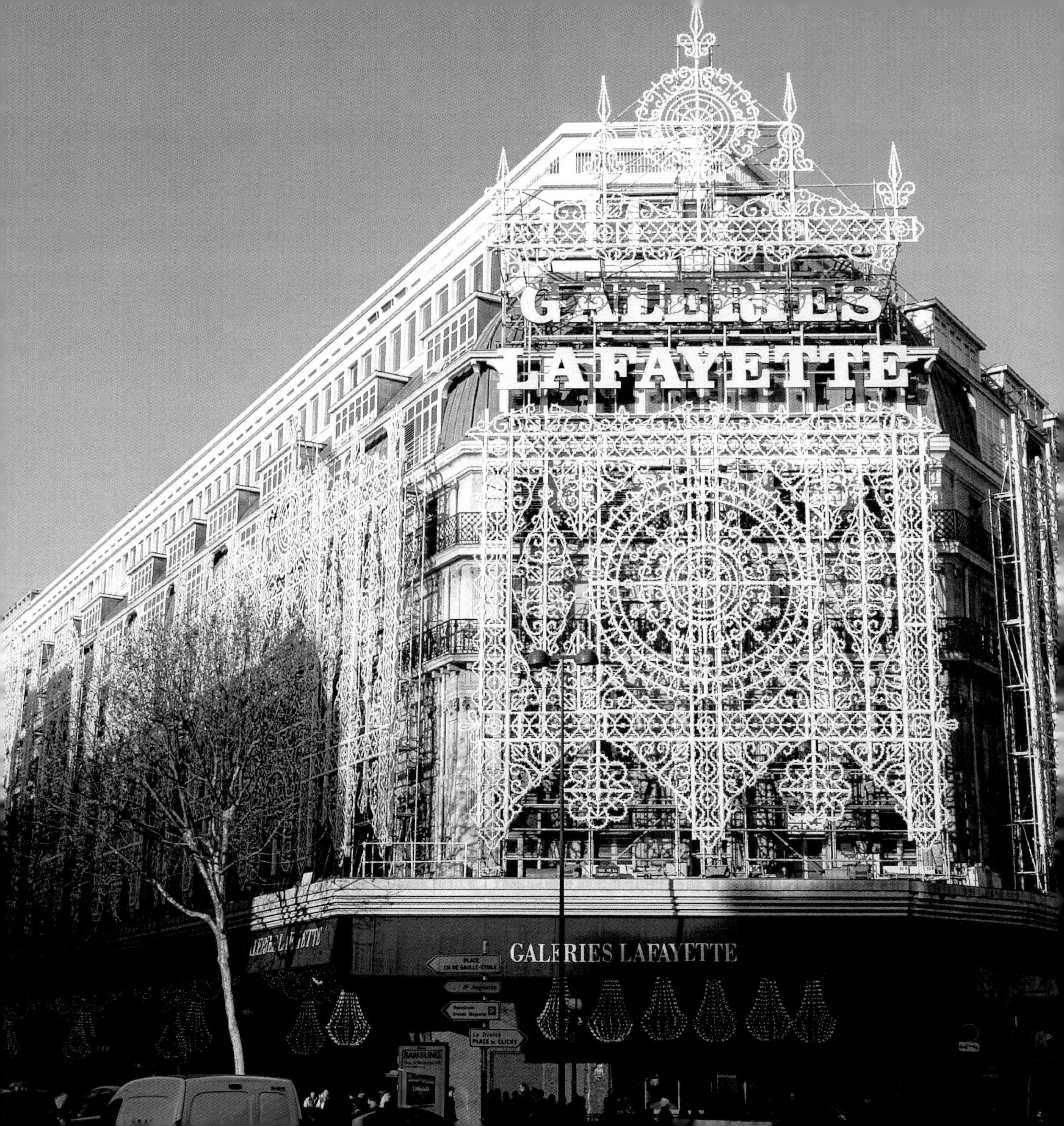
GALERIES
LAFAYETTE
GALERIES LAFAYETTE
SAMSUNG

Made in United States
North Haven, CT
05 December 2024